Connecting with ...

LOVE TALKS

Harshada Pathare

BlueRose Publishers

First Published in January 2020

ISBN: 978-93-89888-09-6

Price: INR 114/-

BLUEROSE PUBLISHERS
www.bluerosepublishers.com
info@bluerosepublishers.com
+91 8882 898 898

Cover Design:
Mohd Arif

Typographic Design:
Namrata Saini

Distributed by: BlueRose, Amazon, Flipkart, Shopclues

Dedicated

to

Cats

About the Author

A weaver

An astute observer of everything

Harshada connects via words…

How intriguing it is: the notion of words as an art-form, and writing as a manifestation of one's dreams. Harshada embraces this philosophy, connecting art to daily life, threading her stories with magic. Every writer is unique, and that is the essence that scripts every writer. Some writers see themselves as simple storytellers, some as conveyors of knowledge. Others as artists identify. There is no traditional definition, but everyone should strive to discover the craft within them—the craft with immortal output.

Celebratory and mystic, Love Talks is the embodiment of that passion. These poems will more than entertain. They'll push you; too, along a path that enters the eternal. These poems will inspire you on your way, and give you insight into the craft of weaving words that get you thinking—maybe get you loving...

Harshada has set her sights on a grander goal. She aims to elevate the craft to art's elusive peaks. Those that have visited her top-tier editorial sites and harshadapathare.com will be familiar with this dedication.

Interested to connect with Harshada's insightful writing?

Follow her on social media.

Don't remain a stranger!

Foreword

Transcending time and space, Harshada Pathare's *Love Talks*, takes the reader from the cosmic to the intimate, from the swirling abstract to the mundane concrete, in words both lofty and accessible. Forging connections between the ephemeral and everyday experience, Pathare's poems guide the reader to connect the overwhelmingly celestial above us with the overlooked simplicity surrounding us.

Galaxies, flowers, relationships, and the depths of the human soul are all vehicles to carry a timeless awareness of love and love's overarching reign over all creation. Whether personal love of another incarnation of humanity or one soul's love of the infinite, Pathare writes of the vast interconnectedness of all things, all times, all beings.

Simultaneously individualistic and humble—a part of existence's measureless whole—these poems reflect the human duality that makes life painful, ecstatic, and worth living. Each poem is inward-looking and outward-reaching, intent to connect with other souls. There is attention to the infinite sand that pours through an unbounded hourglass, and there is focus on each unique grain.

Linger, then, and listen to Love Talks. Reflect on the murmurings of our own hearts and souls, adrift in the immeasurable, joining the fires of our own emotion.

Prof. Robert Masterson
November 2019
New York City, New York, USA

Contents

Night Walk

Nights are out in full swing,
And my heart is a moving song,
Let's go for a walk in your favorite spots

Where souls freeze in deep memories
Where love pleads to love for consuming
Winds drift closer and closer to interrupt
From skies, stars crouch down to see,
Fascinating shots filled with suspense

Lost in fragrant rose beaches and wild berries,
I feel we are the King and Queen of stories
Far off, I could hear the owl agreeing with me,
Walking in, and out we are dreaming on the streets

Love irresistibly blooms in the pool of moonlight,
The most beautiful walk can illuminate a lifetime
The glances, whispers, scents cluster as light falls,
To create memories that can be prefaced with words,
"I remember the most beautiful night walk in …"

Coffee Talk

Coffee is great,
It knows how to weave your way,
And floods the air with happy omens

A vibrant glance clears clouds away,
Makes its way through crowded eyes

An emotional lawn takes us on an adventure,
I carefully poured my dreams into the cup

Sips of coffee made my smile sweeter,
My heart stood straight like a tightly held flower

Savoring soft, sweet sips is like a musical symphony,
Sparks a gripping desire to create a sensational rhapsody

Hours slowly moved ahead like a waving flag,
I swayed up and down to excavate complexities

The sight of brewing coffee is a fulfilling promise,
To look back and again relish the passing time

In a cup of coffee, I swallowed your entire history,
And my mighty pen stole blank papers to spill…

Love Walks

A long time ago,
When you and I wandered in far-flung galaxies,
For millions of miles to find a perfect spot to colonize
We loved each other till outlines dimmed

We spoke for so many light-years, sitting close,
And learned the knack of arranging universe
We talked endlessly in an open, galactic center
Made magnificent studies about each other
As you spoke, your sharp features sparkled,
And in your blue eyes shiny meteors streaked

It is a true spectacle to see how spiraled galaxies,
Slowly create stars and bars with soft hands,
Throw up a colorful cast to close black holes
Some of it got absorbed, some reflected back

In the live orchestra of spinning galaxies,
Our hearts weaved poetry as we moved
We went higher and higher holding a flare,
Striking the ascension chords in space

It is so interesting to watch the cave people,
And drizzle over them interstellar confetti
Roaming here we found the spilled secret,
Even galaxies merger to create galaxies

As we both walked and talked,
To explode space with our words and acts
Galaxies teamed up to hear and see our love-talks

A Rose in Love

A rose comes with many thorns,
Like me and my multiple flaws
The signature of a rose is its beauty,
But for me it is my strength, not body

Like each masterpiece, a rose takes time to blossom,
It evolves slowly, softly to become a flower of stardom
Breaking aside the thorns, it stands in full loveliness,
Even in darkness, my heart is bright and full of surprises
Deep down in every rose lies a heart covered with snow,
Never spoken, never heard, it lingers there, waiting to glow
Looking at the sun, it reveals the deepest
secret that no one knows,
"You are the dream I love to see in the night,"
it whispers in sorrow

The face of the rose turns to the sky as
it sways in the breath of air,
Glistening in the shower of sunrays, '
it wonders where the stars are'
In the deepest nights, it waits to be lifted and
pressed in a book,
The cries of the rose telling a story in silence
and the silence will speak

It speaks of quiet and loud emotions,
Shows shades of dark and light
Shows shyness and boldness standing,
At the edge of both the worlds
Infinite layered petals open up to expose
The divine parts that crave life,
It takes only a flower as complex as the rose
To contain a universe inside it

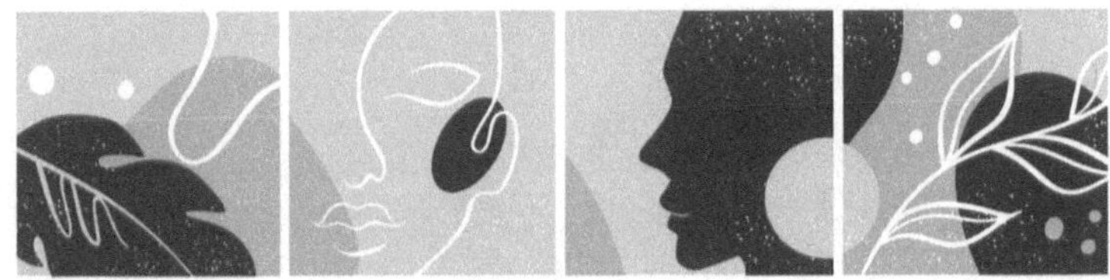

A Woman is Born

She aroused from the roundness of moon,
A kind of divinity, a kind of beauty
Until the earth drew a path to bring her down,
As all waters of creation would spring from her
She would weave love with threads drawn from hearts,
Roots sunk deep in the womb and hearts soaring to the sky

A spectacular tree of life, love, and sacredness,
She dances lightly with certain coyness
Stretching up to hide her face in the blueness,
Her energy rekindles as she feels the naturalness

Filled with the brilliance of spring, buds, and birds,
The earth looks far superior to heavens
It is her loving presence that imagines and creates,
With open and outstretched wings, she ascends

Love, beauty, divinity is embedded in women,
Each snowflake is a perfect crystal made in heaven
It isn't a theory, she is the glorious beginning
And without her, it would be not the same story

Love-Talks

Talks with you are like desserts,
Even a small chat satisfies my heart
Each talk forges a new path,
Be in whatever mood it is full of spark

I love to listen to your stories and conversations,
Deeply intertwined with anxieties and emotions
Speaking with flutters, feelings and foresights,
I am promoting your new expression styles

A strong yet simple interaction full of insights,
Cultivating deeper and richer levels of intimacy
I admire the way you didn't let sadness dim your light,
I appreciate how you hard-wired yourself to be optimistic

The hidden scars on my soul become wings to soar,
Above the isles of beauty, titling over the freshness
I thank you, as a cheerful, stronger, and better person,
Is born every day from the seeds of your loving words

I want to keep going the legacy of talks to communicate,
The infinite, unconditional, and all-encompassing love
I leaned back to recollect how your simple, practical talks,
Actually made good sense in life's hardest moments

No smith had the knack of hammering me to grow in life,
No bridge could ever stride if it wasn't made of your voice
I am now made up of strong bones ready for any season,
Your pull released the aspiring plumage of my clipped soul
Even when you were not around like the
North Star in the sky,
Your words echoed in my mind to open
up a multitude of ways

Love of the Soul

In the eternal cycle of collapse and creations,
I incarnated a thousand times with pleasure
To share timeless stories of love from coast to coast,
And light up the universe with a thousand suns

I oscillated with numerous souls as they made love,
In search of a strong hand to hold me from being tossed
Where others narrowed to trim or took to greater strides,
I sensed a steering body with an offering of true insights

Souls that were unknown are now linked to us by strings,
But my heart blossomed like a flower as you came nearer
I was waiting for a soul-mate that would make me complete,
Walk upon the way of greater peace
and unimagined beauties

My love brought me a special gift of
never-before-seen sunrise,
The sun rose in my eyes as tears
dropped with mixed emotions
My love is so romantic, we filled endless
stars in the dark nights,
It made us believe we are divine and
human at the same time

These discoveries of love will be
sacred stories for tomorrow,
May more and more souls come to
hear lessons and realize
That beauty and flesh are nothing
but lifeless, abstract images,
True love lies in some other compound
that make up the soul

Our World of Love

The whole little world that we both created,
Slowly infused life as our breaths sparked
Our love spins and swivels in perfect alignment,
As we ascend and descend in the waters deep

The columns of fire blaze the world,
Covering the landscape in black for no one to see
Roaring on the heights, nothing can exhaust light,
Traces of lingering smoke want to do the fire dance
To create another primordial spark in someone's heart

Our impulse oscillates backward and forward,
The million threads of my heart hooked at your end
I have signed for an entire life an unbreakable bond,
With a willingness to continue in our next avatars

We spoke only of love and acted only on love making,
And in the virtue of that precious, infinite moment,
We made the sun, moon, stars, and universes small,
And filled them with emotions, words, and sounds to tell,
The story of our love that slices heaven in day and night
It was just an ordinary fire made up from our glances

I am the Gallery

I am the powerful madness that believes,
It is better to be crazy than to be boring
I like to be perfect and stay the best,
Whenever I make a mistake, I do laugh
And simply quote a poem to move on
I laugh loudly and it does irritate people around,
It seems as if they are living and dead at same time

They tried to manipulate me and make me a prisoner,
Follow the herds and never say any contrarian words
You can't tame me for I am the madness that creates,
A little sanctuary for myself to explore and fidget
I am fully-fledged and love to paint besides the lamp-light,
Lots of books, strokes of paints that never left indoors

I am harsh on the canvas when in deep pain,
I write and speak words, as I am not born in silence
People do criticize, analyze, and condemn me,
They think I am a spider in an ambit of stars
But it is from a spider the art of weaving descended,
A spider has innate skills to make silk threads,
Spin them in nifty patterns of radials and orbs

I have a good set of values yet break some rules,
It is not that I am an unprincipled crook,
But sometimes I do patch with sensible lies
I believe in an empty, dark universe,
Made up of chaos, sounds and waves
But I also believe in a God that molds,
The universe into a living abode for the insane

Pull out the bubble wrap, see the leaning canvas
Look around the paintings that speak my stories
I am the GALLERY... breathing the paints and pain

LOVE

Word-Struck

The day ended in soft lights and poetry,
Leaving in me the endless urge to write about you
There is no flattery, no pretending but true words,
That need to be spun to create a universe about you

Words are flowing in natural and bold hues,
As I exorcised my weakness one by one to be strong
The density of your love has swept pride away,
The only thing we create when we are in love is love

I am aligning with you, excavating my whole world,
Falling on the grounds like a mole of beaten dust
As trees grow in heights and on plains my small words,
Now are on an expanse holding enormous feelings

I wrote so long it cracked my fingers bloody,
With ink, sweat and blood, I continued to write,
As there was nothing else that I could then do

I washed my fingers with waves of churning tears,
I cried and cried till the ink changed from blue to white
I knew the tide was coming, as words disappeared slowly,
All of my writings are now buried in the depths of water
I now need to drink the entirety of saltwater to survive,
Now I need to gather enough energy to reach the shoreline

I left my name on the white sand in rhythmic style,
As a reminder to the ocean that love knows to endure
When the tumbling ocean again got quieter,
I started writing words about you on the waters

Did You Never Know?

I have touched you a million times,
Did you ever see the imprints of my touch?

I have imagined you in a million forms,
Did you ever feel the lightning in your heart?

I began to draw you in my private notebook,
Did you ever see the colors splash on your soul?

I started to script delightful stories about you,
Did you ever think you were becoming someone's story?

I have expressed my feelings in silence many times,
Did you ever sense a lonely heart longing to love?

I have sung a love song for you every midnight,
Did you ever hear the rhythms floating on the breeze?

I have seen you in the sunsets and sunrises,
Did you ever feel the spark to recreate someone's life?

I have sent you countless kisses till my lips got dry,
Did you ever get drenched in sweet, white waters?

I have crossed your path many times to see your smile,
Did you ever notice a welcome sign tattooed somewhere?

I have proposed to you innumerable times,
Did you receive these million messages that seek an answer?

Mood Struck

Like water bodies, my mood swings,
To and fro, back and forth,
Creating a quirky universe unlike usual
Gravity creates high and low tides,
Else pulls me on the other side
From shore, my mind pushes me out to sea

I meditate upon the calm waters
Heal my soul with rocks and crystals
The sun, breeze, and moon, relax my moods
I dig up the heavens to find my lost peace,
Even beneath the earth it is not buried

I create a dance to vibrate like the universe,
Feel the pulse of divine consciousness moving around,
In one breath I explored the wilderness of forest,
In one sip I swallowed the persistence of the river Nile

Immersed in a deep trance, I dissolved in the infinite,
Recreating and creating from the energy of the divine
Engrossed in the cosmic act of swirling in galaxies,
The ecstasy transformed my simple life into sacred art
The spirited, playful dance completely moulded me,
From a swinging momentum to a creative manifestation

Power Talks

Grass never dreams,
To reach the height of trees
Yet lays in the side,
Bathing in sun, rain, snow, winds

Both have made many journeys together,
In the night, they have heard countless singings and stories
Grass makes in the world a small, bubbling entry,
Tumbling and foaming in the thundering, shivering
It digs deeper against the powerful, driving winds,
Even when snow descends it jumps out to make spring

Each grass is a great column of love and strength,
Humming even when forces of nature are worse
Swaying in liveliness, they rose up to touch the sky,
Pinned to ground yet laughing and leaping to sprint
Thinking of the great stretch ahead of others to explore,
They clap aloud with their thousand hands to inspire

Make me a Child Again

I cannot go back to the toys,
Or live this life of richness and elegance
I cannot go back to the meadows,
Or travel frequently over continents

Where majestic beauties wrapped me in bosom,
When I crept out of our close and lonely home
I love the place where my mind is free to roam,
Rocks and soil are near to soak hands and feet
I nestle in nature, drawing energy from roots and grains,
Even today, the sky remains my best companion

Wind blowing over rivers, plains, and colorful florets,
I want to dip my fingers in rain-soaked thickets
See the sunset over the polished marble deserts of Egypt,
Maple trees spark fire when I lovingly kiss in secret
Let the prophets, poets, and preachers write their thoughts,
For me, nature beholds an eternal promise of strength

I am grown, learned, and sophisticated,
Yet the fragrance and virtues of nature enchant me
I still love to sit on branches of oak, maple, and pine,
Play pranks, find delight in small things, and sleep tight
The craft that makes the world is our prayers and play,
Make me a child again to redesign the world with my clay

Story-Weaver

You have everything in you
A treasure trove of countless stories,
Filled with converging maps, secrets, and symbols
That will live on in the mists of time

You have everything in you
Torrential rains from centuries filling freshwater,
Brimming with stories of reefs, shallows, and storms
Dancing with the gleaming sunbeams on walls

You have everything in you
Skies filled with migrating springs and birds,
Disappearing over the horizon in boundless space
Studded with countless flashing stars telling their names

You have everything in you
A mind filled with stories that makes a library,
Your beautifully expressed ideas turn into breathtaking pages
As we disappear in the mystic depths of infinity

Good vs Bad

There is good, there is bad,
Both exist as yin and yang

Give good to the good,
They deserve the goodness

As Karma goes round and round,
The bad will suffer for their deeds

You reap what you sow is the nature's clause,
The Universe will judge you on your goodness and badness

I learned these divine mantras from ancestors,
All scriptures remind us of these two components

There is some good in us and some bad in us,
But the good in us should always overpower the bad in us
The Universe doesn't except each of us to be saints or gurus,
The most we can be is a good human
being of virtues and values

Spark the candle of goodness, share kindness wherever you go,
Even if you encounter the bad,
give them your good with a smile
Maybe they will savor the taste and share the recipe,
And then, the bad will have to find another market to sell

Our Love Continues

Let me first say the true things,
"You are the best thing that happened to me,
Only because of you, I felt the inner need to create
We understand each other like the moon and tide,
Only you brought to life my deepest feelings."

One is infinite heavens, another is uplifting harmonies,
Together we hold within us countless love stories
Make me a potter to caress your unformed clay,
Let me be a sculptor to chisel you to perfection,
Like a poet, let me ink for you an aspect of perception

My energy is opening in varying depths to change your hues,
We are deeply engulfed, and don't know who is skin and soul

I still remember the first time I saw you,
I tried a million times but could never forget you
I wanted to stop myself but couldn't force myself,
My feelings grew stronger and stronger for you
Wrapped in your love, now I am more empathic,
Your offerings of love made me extraordinary

The love we make in our deepest meditations,
Reaches us on the shore where rests calm waves
Continuing our love as time collapses and expands,
I feel the essence and beat of an unborn love-song

This is Me

I am an unspoken ocean,
My waves are overlapping words
Partly made up of sun and moon,
I am a mixture of salt and water

I am endless but not expressionless,
When my words stride, even maps slide
I am silent but not without a voice,
When my mood disrupts, volcanoes erupt

I am moving from one place to another,
Leaving a goodbye kiss on each shore
I have crossed all the boundary lines,
You cannot tame my free mind and open spirit

I spend countless hours watching outlines of nature,
It feels I am touching infinity with my bare hands
I carry stories of sweat, salt, and blood, from centuries past
Only I know the secret of how to make the shores happier

I am filled with treasures, nature, and mysteries,
These are embodiments of my bursting creativity
Plunge down to the depths of my wavering soul,
To know the openness and vastness of my body

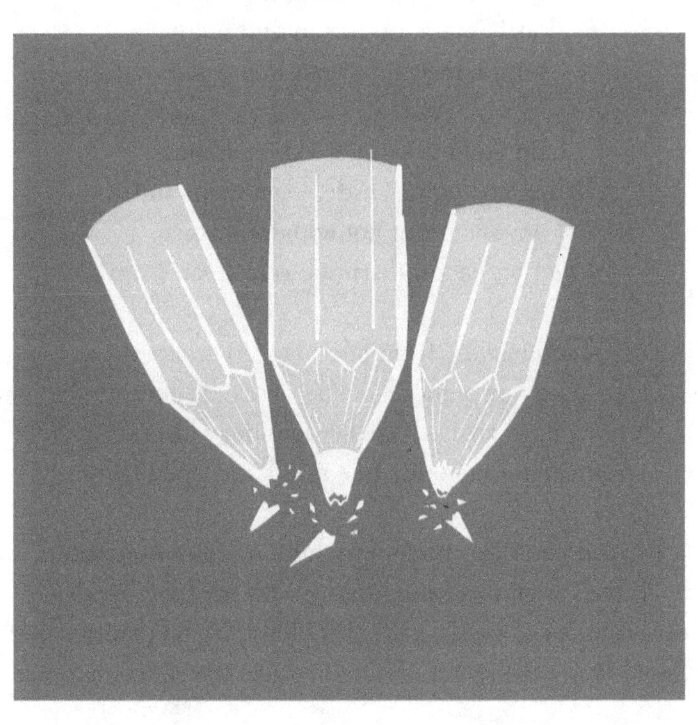

My Mistakes

I made big mistakes, sometimes even great mistakes,
It does not mean I will stop, hide, and grovel in shame
Sometimes wisdom slips from my mind making nonsense,
I stare at the blank pages, thinking how to further navigate

Why can I not make mistakes?
I am a woman, a human with a heart and brain
I am a cosmic power, manifesto of God's love
I am growing every day, learning from my mistakes
I am learning every day, enriching from the past

Sugar and salt perfectly complement each other,
Mistakes and success blend richer experiences
I don't deserve punishment or sessions for few wrongs,
I am thriving with pride, living with integrity, is it not
enough?

Pin my mistakes upon my soul,
So their brilliance remains timeless
Motionless, breathless,
I won't lie down like a silent musical instrument

But will weave melodious harmonies,
To discover a new musical masterpiece
Each of my musical recordings,
Will be unique, uplifting and powerful

Each mistake is a connecting stem,
Opening leaves of a new possibility
The message hidden beneath each mistake,
Is simple to be understood,
"I won't stop…" and it is definitely not another mistake…

Lover of a Broken Heart

Your broken heart for me,
Is a unique piece of art
The most beautiful thing,
That opened my eyes to wonder
I rolled the kaleidoscope,
To see amazing colors and designs
Creatively made by the gleaming glints,
Of your shattered and torn parts

Your heart is so filled,
With love and feelings of affection
Give it to someone who knows,
It is a treasure and not trash

How could someone throw it?
To break into a million pieces
Did the loud noise not shake,
The space to create another Big Bang?
Did the sobs and heart-breaking pain,
Not pierce the stillness of silent nights?
Did the universe turn so deaf to ignore it?
And spread out the flashy stars to light skies

I want to pull you out of the darkness to glow,
May be it would need lots of time and efforts
But I am willing to heal your darkest depths,
And stitch your heart again with beautiful threads

I am an artist in love with fragments and pieces,
Allow me to create the most beautiful mosaic design
I'll patch my cracks with olden tales and songs,
What pieces that remain I'll rearrange to let in the sun

Made up of fragments

I am made up of fragments,
Some proportion of stars, light and dark matter
Each fragment inside me expands to become,
An individual galaxy bursting with sparks of life

I hung the sun and moon above my head,
Like white clouds towering to high heavens

The flooding lights invoked mysteries of divinity,
I am lost in the roaring chaos, thundering skies
Universes sank and rose, trembling in deep pain,
Echoes descended upon the pitch as songs of fate

I discovered inside myself a hidden portal of special powers,
There, I could seek wisdom, philosophy, and even happiness
I felt true companionship, on entering that unknown land,
Like a pigeon swooped fast to the canyon of opening glory

A celestial being adorned with flesh, I entered the earth,
To breath, thrive, and yearn for the divine elixir of life
The emotion and expression that I spoke of was longing,
Those in rags and even fine cloaks have experienced, too

Where is my love?

"Where is my love?"

I questioned in a loud, bold voice
Looking at the never-ending celestial heights
I asked the Gods of oracles and prophecies
To strip me of everything, as it is a flawed glory,
Except love, there is nothing that really exists

I stand between the edges of two infinities,
Piercing the depths to search for an atom of life
For ages I stand, seeing visions and hearing voices,
Trying to interpret the enigmatic mysteries

The sound of my breathing whipped the relentless silence,
In the infinite moments, spirals and circles expand
As I introspect inside the story of the stories,
Colors disappear as reality and fantasy blend

As I ascend higher in the azure depths,
Curtains pull over the vast, dark terrains
With hope, I cross the stellar distances and fiery depths,
To reach the point where natural and supernatural meet

I wait in complete loneliness in a human body,
Melting and waiting to see you in perfect harmony
Every vibe looks for your face in infinity,
Universal pillars loom over my prayers in an intricate pattern
I swept the belt of infinite universes and burning suns,
Only to discover your fingerprints on the turf of cosmic sand

I Propose Love

Falling into the deep wells of eternity,
Like a sunbeam fallen from glorious skies
I am a lover, passionate to drink your love,
Half-created and half-perceived by your soul

I am only longing to behold you in this life-time,
For so many years, I am waiting in these massifs
To gift you the ancient heritage of my blood and love,
From the truths of my emotions descends moving songs

I need more numbers to make the count now infinite,
I could stop breathing, as it exhausts me but not loving
In moonlight, my soul rouses to express boundlessness,
Every night a star, burns out as I wait for you in darkness
All I see is your face at daybreak and nightfall without fail,
This is how a pilgrim wanders on the pilgrimage of love,

I wrote verses of love on clouds, dew, snow, frost, and rains,
As the dew falls on leaves, let my love run in your veins
In your eyes shines the smaller version of infinite heavens,
In every breath you will hear syllables that make your name
When all lie half asleep and half-awake
in a dreamy state of mind,
I assume the form of the moon to
dream of an irresistible union

Love-Bearer

I will carry the scent of love,
To far-off places and distant shores
Overcoming the languid heat and storms,
Cracking cold seasons and torrential rains

Leaving behind a trail for lovers to venture,
Creating another breed to inspire emotions
I love to be an honest medium to write stories,
And create the most romantic love journal to read

Spreading love over long stretches of sand and snow,
Crossing fences and trenches to spout mortal boundaries
Pulling millstones of love to grind to finer particles,
Whirling love-dust on fields and gardens to bloom

Sending sparks of life to rekindle ashes of love,
Opening the seal to share miraculous secrets
I am inspiring people to blossom in all seasons,
Like love that never knows any beginnings or ends

Half of the world is now lost in the delight of fragrance,
For the other half, I am still carrying in my dusty palms,
The musk that bears fragrance from where love originates

Warrior of Words

I made wings of confidence,
From feathers of failures
Making sadness disappear in air,
As I weaved smooth rhythms out of it

I have learned to be a mistress of my own,
And even wore a breastplate to protect my heart
Time mocked but I believed in my strength,
And continued to embody hope in my crippled life

I never collected antiques or luxuries or status symbols,
Only necessities of life and stories that stir hearts
Words are the inner longings, like breath to the body,
Living in the world of words, I have kept everything nameless

Sometimes few of my words broke into fragments,
I have kept them hidden from darkness, moon, and owls
The battle for survival and freedom still goes on every day,
The only weapon I behold is the ink of my pain and grit

Art of the full moon

Full moon night is the call of love,
To illustrate love-making without fear
The bright, round, full moon leads lovers,
As ever-growing passion mounts upon them

The full disc hangs upon the wheeling dark expanse,
Torturing lovers till they reach a point of madness
Stars intermingle to create a romantic arrangement,
As the treading nightfall infuses faithfulness and craving

In the moon and stars' dark sky, lovers leave imprints,
As they magnificently discover a part of another person
With every motion in night, moving bodies and voices harvest
The wind plays harp music orchestrated with a million
fireflies,
As they flash on and off to create the perfect prologue

The moon, still in its everlasting youth, looks at lovers,
The darkness of the night enhances their endless celebrations
There is something human about the moon as it connects,
In different meaningful forms, it has an emotional pull
There is something divine about the moon as it shines,
In the nights it creates a world of spiritual essence

I am a goddess

I am an evolving Goddess learning how to play,
Awakening my powers to live boldly like waves

I mold my imagination to craft new manifestations,
No one else except experience is the best preceptor

I open my heart to express love and goodness,
Immerse the earth with streams of abundance and kindness

I may not be so beautiful to make hearts sizzle,
Yet my courage and enthusiasm set so many of them on fire

I know the value of gratitude and the power of positivity,
As these are the tools that make me stronger every day

I smile in pain and thrive to heal others with compassion,
For karma will answer they who have obstructed my way

I trust only my intuition and live in an authentic style,
Like fire, water, earth, sky, and ether, I am expanding,

My energy rises up like a whirlwind towards heavens
I am born to be a legend somewhere in the celestial heights

My terrestrial identity is made up of flesh, stardust and water,
Seeing me, even Goddess Venus feels she needs a little
makeover

Unspoken Words

No one will ever know of our unspoken love,
Which bound us together without any vows
It continues to grow like a beanstalk in a story,
I can feel the intimacy even without kissing

In the glamour of twilight, feelings scatter across skies,
I trembled in fear as my voice could not converse
The passion of unspoken words can spark flames,
It becomes a raging inferno trapped in my soul

In every waking moment the words,
Pretend to sleep to avoid breaking open
In the world of changing emotions,
I am full of unspoken words

When the eyes are closed to express,
The lonely heart brims with flooding waters
Sometimes lips desire to slide and speak,
Messages of an unspoken tear about to trickle
The mind intricately weaves a token of unspoken tapestry,
No music, no drums, no songs but rhythms soar

In the air floats our million unvoiced words,
Left uncradled like lullabies across the oceans
Our secret words converge in a deep silence,
To form an unknown bond of unspoken communion

Moonstruck

The moon is out in full swing,
To speak of her lonely stories
She knows flaws, solitude, and sadness,
That is why she loves to walk in darkness

She knows the love and feelings of hearts,
Understands the touching poetry of lovers
She is desperate to embrace the mighty Ocean,
Moving even closer to engulf its crushing waves

Her erotic pull is very intense and moving,
The ocean cannot stop and assumes the form of the tide
Her beauty leaves a lining in the eye of the beholder,
Even the glorious sun cries in deep agony

Her beauty is a timeless poem of the Creator,
Sensual yet shy, she lies open beneath heavenly skies
Of mesmerizing nights she crafts her own vivid portrait,
Every artist looks up at the sky to loosen her lunar strings
Her beauty lends an appetite to followers, the free

Gods disguised in clouds gather to see her eternal beauty,
Her brilliance stretches across the vaults of the entire galaxy
Between heavens, earth and skies, her eyes behold with glory,
In the calm bosom of the ocean she reflects like milk and honey

I watch her every single night until her last slit fades,
And plunge into the sky to collect the love letters she leaves
From her evocative muses, I weaved my poetic inhibitions,
From her powerful aphrodisiacs, I discovered my desires

New Year's Knock

New Year is around the corner,
And my wings are plumed with delight
With the passing year about to end,
Let's lean upon its bosom and recollect

How we walked through the weeds and stones,
With courage in heart and bright smile on lips
When time was low, we became fiery and fierce,
And created a way out of the storms and rains

Interesting guesses about the coming New Year,
Tickle my imagination, sending whispers for the wind
Though it is all written on the skies unknown to us,
We lit lanterns to spark happiness that is hung in heavens

Let New Year give me a little lift to create powerful moments,
Moments that churn life experiences into joyful celebrations
Bless me with deep awakening to decipher hidden meanings,
Let me get up, step out, be the best influence for inspiration
Stitch again the pieces of life with threads of love and passion,
Mingle more with colors as I continue to sketch life on my own

I have learned much about life, people, and the world around,
Now let me create my own story with triumphs and tribulations
The door of New Year is prompting me to open,
With a new soul and new senses, I am coming...